Aella Greene

River, Bird and Star

Aella Greene

River, Bird and Star

ISBN/EAN: 9783744791618

Printed in Europe, USA, Canada, Australia, Japan

Cover: Foto ©Andreas Hilbeck / pixelio.de

More available books at **www.hansebooks.com**

RIVER, BIRD AND STAR

(SECOND EDITION)

BY

AELLA GREENE,

AUTHOR OF
" JOHN PETERS, "GATHERED FROM LIFE," ETC.

PUBLISHED IN 1896.

COPYRIGHT, 1896,
BY
AELLA GREENE.

PRESS OF
THE BRYANT PRINTING COMPANY,
FLORENCE, MASS.

CONTENTS

I.
BEYOND:

II.
HERE AND NOW:

III.
CONTRAST:

IV.
IDYLS OF FREEDOM:

BEYOND

I.

"WHERE THE NOBLE HAVE THEIR COUNTRY."

A BOVE the grandeur of the sunsets
    Which delight this earthly clime,
And the splendors of the dawnings
    Breaking o'er the hills of time
Is the richness of the radiance
    Of the land beyond the sun,
Where the noble have their country
    When the work of life is done!

Speech cannot describe their heaven,
    Nor hath earth such brightness known,
For that heaven is the country
    Of the Mighty and His Throne!
Man's brief furlongs cannot bound it,
    Nor his reason comprehend;
God alone counts all its headlands,
    And like Him it hath no end!

Power almighty flows forever
   Round the wondrous land above,
In its flood and ebbing constant
   To the everlasting love;
Chanting with the matchless cadence
   Of a deep and boundless sea,
To the continent of heaven,
   Anthems of eternity !

Welcome to those glories given
   From angelic harps of gold,
Shall full often be repeated,
   Yet it never shall grow old;
Music grander than earth's noblest,
   Than all eloquence of words
And the sweetest of the carols
   Of the gladdest of the birds.

And those glories shall the problem
   Of this earthly life explain,
All its bitter turn to sweetness,
   All its losses turn to gain.

And the rapture of the new life
　　Shall exceed the griefs of this;
And amid those scenes of grandeur
　　Even labor shall be bliss !

Welcome there, and there forever
　　Free from artifice of earth,
Shall the noble of that country,
　　In its things of real worth,
Read the wisdom of the Father,
　　From whose all-creating hand
Are the beauties, and the glories,
　　And the people of that land.

There they learn what mean the visions
　　Of the ancient seers that tell
Of the wonderful possessions
　　Where the glorified shall dwell,
Of a better heaven than cities,
　　Though of gold and jasper made,
Of a soul delighting country
　　Blessed with hillside, brook and shade.

There, magnificent with forests,
   Is that country of the skies,
Far excelling in its bird-songs
   All the earthly minstrelsies.
And that country hath its mountains
   And is resonant with streams
That are sweeter in their music
   Than the rivers of our dreams !

Blooms of finest form and lustre,
   Fragrant on the eternal hills,
With their odors bless the zephyrs,
   That, harmonious with the rills,
Sing, to give the angels pleasure
   And to welcome there, on high,
The immortals, from their struggles,
   To the glories of the sky !

Yet a higher theme than heaven
   And beyond its vastness far,
Lovelier than its fairest valleys,
   Grander than its mountains are,

Shall the noble have to study;
  For the One of matchless worth,
For the Savior of the sorrowing
  And the sinful of the earth,

With His mission here completed,
  Shall abide with them above,
Far outshining all the wonders
  Of the country of His love.
There He giveth them an entrance
  And that higher work to do
That shall keep them ever growing
  And the charm of living, new !

And His name, throughout the ages,
  As the æons circle by,
To the trend and to the cadence
  Of their own eternity,
Shall be theme and inspiration
  In the land beyond the sun,
Where the noble have their country
  When the work of life is done !

THE JOY OF DOING.

THERE is heaven in grand endeavor;
  Even here it bringeth joy.
O ! the ecstasy of action
  And the bliss of high employ
Where the powers are all untrammeled
  And the soul can breathe the air
Of the country of the spirit—
  O the joy of action there !

There, however great the longing,
  Still the heaven shall be more !
Longs the soul for wide exploring?
  There'll be vastness to explore !
Is there wish for sweetest music ?
  There'll be harmonies on high
Far beyond imagination
  Of the people of the sky !

With the wish and eye for beauty
  Shall be rarest tints to see,

Grouped in combinations painted
   Only in eternity,
Where the limners live to study
   And for centuries have given
Their ambitions to be perfect
   In the tracery of heaven !

BURDEN BEARERS.

COURAGE ! O ye burden bearers,
   Faring upward to the skies !
By the very weights ye carry
   To that country ye shall rise.
Fare ye bravely, burden bearers,
   Fare ye bravely every day;
Angels of that better country,
   Hither winging, guard the way
From marauding spirits vexing
   Pilgrims on the heavenward road;
And if burdens are too heavy,
   Angels aid to bear the load,

And delight with their description
  Of the land beyond the skies.
Courage ! O ye burden bearers,
  To that country ye shall rise !

A HEAVEN.

WHEREVER bloom the happy isles
    In lasting verdure drest,
Whereon perpetual morning smiles
  High welcome to the blest.

No gilded barques bear any there;
  Nor, borne o'er summer seas,
Do any find the orchards fair
  Of the Hesperides.

Wherever the elysium is,
  In what good land afar,

And gained by what high ministries
  Of what benignant star,

It is not reached along the way
  Where sirens charm the sea;
But seek, the warning angels say,
  Through Christ of Calvary,

The kingdom of conditions high,
  Where quality hath rate,
Where fitness, and not heraldry,
  Gives entrance through the gate.

For what man is, not where he is,
  His heaven is, or hell;
His heaven the heavenly qualities
  That prompt his doing well.

His heaven that high ennoblement
  That gives to whom 'tis given,

The blessing of a heart content
  To win his way to heaven.

SIC ITUR AD ASTRA.

THOU selfish one who seekest heaven
  Through fear of final fire,
And never had for heaven itself
  The first sincere desire,

Supreme unselfishness alone
  Can for the skies prepare,
And he alone may hope for heaven
  Who loveth what is there.

Thou asking God to grant the boon
  Thou hast not tried to win,
Beseeching His forgiving grace
  Yet never hating sin,

And ever whining for the heaven
   Where only brave souls are—
Wherever in the realms of space
   Revolves that happy star,

The object of the good man's hope
   And goal of all his quest,
Bright sphere of life, and growth, and joy,
   And work that giveth rest—

That place of earth is nearest heaven
   Where the unselfish dwell,
And where there is but selfishness
   There needs no other hell !

And thou who deemest 'tis decreed,
   By mandate of thy God,
That thou be favored in His sight
   And spared the fateful rod,

Which thou dost think is wholly right
   For those despised by thee,

And therefore doomed by Him to wrath
　　To all eternity,—

It was a fratricide declared
　　His brother not his care,
And he alone is sure of heaven
　　Who leads another there !

Go thou, like Christ, and strive to save
　　Another than thyself ;
For hoarding up salvation is
　　As base as hoarding pelf !

And when, like His, thy life shall bless
　　Thy suffering fellowmen,
Then thou, for heaven canst hope, thyself,
　　But art condemned till then !

FORECASTING.

O THOU who bravely up the path
Which frequent thorn of trouble hath,
      Steadfast didst try,
If upward still thy courage climb
Thy patience shall attain in time
The summit of the height sublime
      From which thine eye,

Unhindered by dense airs that blow
To cloud morass of doubt below,
      Shall see fair ground
Beyond the waters flowing cold,
A country which doth richness hold
Excelling that the men of old
      At Eshcol found.

Some time in exultation spent
Shall intervene ere thy descent
      At beck of sprite
Whose barge shall bear thee o'er the tide

To land thy vision hath descried—
Nor shalt thou always there abide,
      Nor wish thou might.

For, far from false and with the true,
Thy youth renewed and vision new,
      Thou soon shalt be,
To learn from features of that shore
That they but prophesy of more
And bid thine enterprise explore
      With ecstasy

New continent, and seas, and isles,
Whereon such radiant solstice smile
      To cheer thy gaze
That thou shalt think the brightest beams
The former gave, but faded gleams
Of sunshine of forgotten dreams
      Of other days !

That land attained, thy study there
Shall thee for further quest prepare,
      That shall allure ;

And faring on, what thou shalt find
Thy broadened and still growing mind
Shall solve, assimilate and bind,
          And make secure.

And it shall rare nutrition be,
And spur, and stimulant, for thee,
          To aid thy will,
That shall increase with thy desire.
To this new good thou mayst aspire
And mayst attain, to find yet higher,
          To beckon still !

Inspiring faith that paints the scene—
A heaven of hills and valleys green,
          With songsters bright
That sing responses to the call
Of mellow murmuring waterfall ;
And blue, benignant over all,
          A sky of light,

Whose language is not only peace,
But that which teaches an increase
          Of all that's heaven,

In such gradations evermore
As thou shalt inward from that shore
The country of the blest explore,
            With blessing given.

And, scanning copse and forest belt
That through the years of heaven have felt
            The zephyrs' joy
That sweeps the flower-scented plains
Of that good land whose bliss explains
Thine earthly lot, thou'lt hear the strains
            The birds employ

And songs the airs and rivers sing,
To make the elysian valleys ring
            The ages through.
And angels of the loftiest lyre,
In joy that thou shouldst so aspire,
Shall wake the strings to noblest fire
            They ever knew.

O ! grandeur of the land that lies
Away somewhere beyond the skies!
            Beyond earth's dream—

How far beyond the visible
Imagination cannot tell,
Howe'er intensely it may dwell
    Upon the theme !

Thou shalt have sail for broadest seas
And time to solve all mysteries
    Thy search hath spied.
Whatever thine ambition be,
Thou shalt no limitation see ;
Thy time is all eternity,
    Thy scope as wide !

HERE AND NOW

II.

THE EQUAL LOT.

WITH equal hand, impartial Heaven
 Bestows on all, the blessings given
  To cheer the earth.

If birds that bless the morns of spring
Alone at regal courts would sing,
  We might complain.

But everywhere, from hill to shore,
The joyous warblers artless pour
  Their songs for all.

As grateful thine anemones
And all the perfumed potencies
  Thy rose exhales

As odors they of kingly kind,
Empurpled in a palace, find
  The flowers to yield

That grow by royal gardener dressed,
And bloom with smiles of princess blessed,
    On sacred days.

Nor sweeter sound than you or I,
Hears king or Croesus, walking by
    The purling brook ;

Nor, navied in their gilded boats,
Than we embarked in common floats,
    More restful plash

Of wave ; nor surer they to ride
In safety to the haven side
    Of waters sailed.

Nor king than we has sweeter hymn
Of Zephyr ; nor doth Sunset limn
    Diviner west

For king, with hues from heavenly fount ;
Nor nearer is the royal count
    Of stars than thine

To His who outlined nature's plan
And reared the astral arch, to span
    The universe !

AMONG THE TREES.

WHERE nature reigns distinctions fade
    That pride may bring to grove and
        glade,
    To flaunt them there.

Rank has no sway at nature's court,
And fame is there of small import,
    And pelf is scorned.

Impartially, when vernal breath
Proclaims the winter's reign of death
    Is at its end,

The maple buds portend the June,
Whose leaves shall cool the torrid noon
    Of summer time.

To thee as kindly welcome wave
The elms as unto prince they gave
    Who fared that way.

And wild and tender harmony
The pensive pines address to thee
    As unto all,

And breathe balsamic airs of health,
Uncaring for their rank and wealth
    Who seek the boon.

The quiet beauty of the beech
To thee as unto all will teach
    If thou wilt learn,

The loveliness of real worth,
Whatever station in the earth
    The worthy have.

To thee as grand the oaks that hold
Discourse with crags of mountain bold,
    Anent the storms.

As unto royalty they seem ;
And for thine eyes as brightly gleam
    The autumn woods

As for the monarch who desires
To imitate their gorgeous fires
    On robes he wears,

But finds that futile is the sleight
Of kings to deck themselves as bright
          As nature shines !

Contrasting with the snowy lands,
As sombre-hued the hemlock stands
          To symbolize

Thy grief, as though the dark cold green,
Sighing, bemoaned with northland queen,
          Her consort dead.

And when, again, the trees in bloom
Dispel the thoughts of death and doom,
          And hope inspire,

Thou canst the graceful tasseling
That decks the birchen boughs of spring
          As well enjoy

Uncrowned, untitled and unknown,
As though instated on a throne
    Of kingly power.

THE LESSON OF THE LILIES.

NATURE rebukes presumptuous men,
    And yet invites the constant ken
    Of reverent souls.

And still the words the Master saith,
Who came of old from Nazareth,
    Nature repeats :

Consider thou the lilies well,
O man, who thinkest thou canst tell
    Their coloring,

And canst the processes divine
Wherein the primal hues combine
　　That beauty give,

And tell the fragrances that meet
To make those rarest odors sweet
　　That lilies shed.

Consider thou the lilies well,
O man, who thinkest thou can tell
　　What lilies are—

Perfection of the alchemies
Wherein the chemists of the skies
　　Have wrought their best !

And lilies not alone meant He
Who taught, on nills of Galilee,
　　Their loveliness.

But all the flowers that decked the field
For Him did sweetest pleasures yield,
    And theme for thought.

And, eloquent above thy speech,
The flowers will still their ethics teach,
    O man of earth,

As when, to prove His doctrine true,
In Palestine, the Teacher drew
    From nature's store.

And, mortal, thou canst ever find,
If well instructed is thy mind
    By heavenly power,

Such high renewal of thy might,
Such inspiration and delight,
    And rest, and peace,

In thinking on the works of God,
From tiny twig and velvet sod
    To mountain peak,

As thou in thine ambitious schemes
Fulfilled unto thy brightest dreams,
    Canst never find !

THE SINGING OF THE BROOKS.

T HE sweetest songsters carol
    Among the Berkshire hills,
In harmony with music
  Arising from the rills
That flow with silvery murmur,
  In melody along
And charm as if in heaven
  They learned the art of song,
And were by Him empowered
  Who formed the starry spheres

And guides their rhythmic motion
  Through all the circling years.

Bright brooks! they came from heaven,
  To teach the tuneful art,
And woo men from their sorrows
  And from their cares apart ;
To teach them high behavior,
  And gentle ways and true,
Inspiring them with courage
  To fight life's battles through ;
The while, through all the harshness
  That gives to earth its ban,
They live attuned for living
  Where harmony began.

There other brooks, in chorus
  With other birds, shall sing,
To tell the power and goodness
  Of the Eternal King ;
And welcome home the singers
  From the dissonance of time

To the melodies of heaven
  And the zephyrs of the clime
With song far, far exceeding
  The music of the rills
That carol with the songsters
  Among these restful hills.

MESSAGES OF THE WATERS.

I

THY valleys how lovely, thy mountains
    how strong,
O Northland, how charming thy rivers of
    song !
No finer through storied lands singeth the
    tide
Of Tiber, or Danube, or Severn, or Clyde ;
No brighter to Scotchmen the burns which
    they know
That sweet to Loch Katrine through heather
    bloom flow ;

No gladder to Lomond whirl joyous away
The streamlets through dingles with hazel
    bloom gay,
Nor sweeter to Switzers sing brooks to
    Lucerne
Than waters whose music New Englanders
    learn.
No sweeter the far wave than waters that sing
Where Greylock of hilltops is grandly the
    king,
Than whirl from Wahconah the waters away,
That bright over gravel of gold and of gray,
Through Dalton dales dimple, and sparkle,
    and play,
Than brooks from Katahdin, than others that
    flow
Where airs from Monadnock inspire them to
    go—
Than sing the bright thousands of brooklets
    along
Entrancing the whole of New England with
    song !

Or, if streamlet is sought of sorrow to tell,

What brook is more plaintive in old country
   dell
Than waters from Monument Mountain that
   purl,
Lamenting the fate of the Indian girl
Who loved where she might not, and thought
   she must die,
And plunged in despair from a precipice
   high.
But sorrow chimes not with the note of your
   voice,
O waters of Northland, that ever rejoice,
And even when warning that danger is near
Intone the monitions to cadence of cheer.

Ye brooks of New England that carol like this,
O warble forever to Northland your bliss !
And ye who admire them, O leave them to run,
And wimple, and sparkle, and sing in the sun,
Unchained to carved channels that dullards
   have made
In worship of Use and the tyrant of Trade !
O leave them that faring unfettered along,
They babble their beautiful blessing of song !

But more than the music or glance of the wave
O'er which every lover of beauty may rave,
While men of each land of their home rivers
    boast
O'er waters enchanting the foreigner's coast
'Tis the truth of their numbers that giveth
    the worth
To musical waters that gladden the earth.

Go, zephyrs of heaven and fleet ye afar
By light of morn lustre and gleaming of star,
And tell in the city, and desert, and dell,
To all who in cot or in palace may dwell,
Or tent on the plains, or anywhere live,
What calm and what rapture the river songs
    give—
The strength for brave doing, the power to
    endure,
The vision to see and the faith to secure
The blessings that nature delights to confer
On those who in loyalty seek them of her.
And mortal, whatever the cadences be
Of rivulet, lake wave, or surge of the sea,

'Tis the spirit of God speaks through them
        to thee.
Who often discovers that man is untrue,
May think that the waves will be false to
        him, too.
Yet faithful forever the voice of the tide !
And, chant they to warn thee, or hearten, or
        guide,
Believe in the waters—a brook never lied !

Or purling as soft as the peace of the sky,
Or singing as grand as the harpers on high,
It giveth forever the essence of truth
That solaces age and sanctifies youth,
And, warbled in valley or prattled in glen,
Is simple as childhood yet equal to men—
Truth sweet as the   roses that blossom in
        heaven,
Truth hither for mortals to rivulets given,
And sung in the sun time and star time, to
        give
High hint and good helping sublimely to live !
What rashness of pride that ventures to spurn,

What wisdom of reverence that listens to
    learn,
The truth to be heard in the song of the burn.
Sweet pleading with Power to be true and be
    mild
As brook is, or bird is, or Christ, or a child,
It telleth the way to the destinies grand
As fancy can paint or wish to command.

Whatever thy talent, what work doth engage,
And living wherever, in whatever age,
And however many thy years on the earth,
The rivulet's voice will still have its worth.
And when shall appear the swift coming day
When thou from this province must journey
    away
To country, wherever that country may be,
Reached over what mountain and over what
    sea,
Where thou shall find much that is strange
    unto thee,
How sweet, when departing, to look on the
    wave

That joy to the days of thine earthly life gave!
And O ! what a rapture 'twill add to thy
    heaven
If there, in that country, like music be given,
If there, to enchant thee, shall carol and
    gleam
The waters with sparkle and song like the
    stream
Enhancing the days of thy sojourning here
With song that is wisdom and song that is
    cheer !

Thy valleys how lovely, thy mountains how
    strong !
O Northland ! how charming thy rivers of
    song !
Bright waters, that winding from Windsor
    away,
Swift purling o'er gravel of gold and of gray,
Through Dalton dales dimple, and wimple,
    and play,
As waters in elfinland singing to fay,
The fairies entrancing as rivulets may,

And rivulets will, so the fairy folks say,
With witcheries weird of the gambolings gay,
And cadences fine and melodies sweet,
And fit where elite of the fairy folk meet,
With honors the princes of elfland to greet—
Ye waves from Wahconah through thickets
    that flow,
And charm to their sweetness the wild
    flowers that grow—
What numbers, bright waters, your music
    can tell,
Thus witching through wildness and dulcet
    in dell !
Sweet waters ! bright waters, that charmingly
    sing
Of Dalton, the jewel of Berkshire the king !

Ye waters, that winding from Windsor away,
Through Dalton dales dimple, and wimple
    and say
As, bright over gravel of gold and of gray,
Ye chant in high music while charmingly gay.
" Thou listening entranced o'er the musical
    wave,

To honor the music, O mortal, be brave ;
Be more than the mood that comes of mere
    charm ;
The trancement of sweetness is cause for
    alarm—"
Ye waters inspiring the valiant until,
Grown godlike from heeding the song of a rill,
They honor in action the truth of the song
That sparkles and warbles their life ways
    along—
What seer hath the vision, ye waves, to divine
The wealth of your wisdom, ye waters benign!

Ye brooks from Katahdin and streamlets that
    flow
Where airs from Monadnock inspire them to
    go ;
Ye waters that sing in Otsego and shine
Reflecting the love of the spirit benign ;
Ye brooks to Itasca that sing through the
    plains,
Entrancing the vastness with charm of your
    strains ;

Ye waters the depths of wild canyons that
    dare,
And calmly the truth to the mountains
    declare—
Wherever all over the Northland ye sing,
From heaven, bright waters, your music ye
    bring !

Ye waters of Northland, that carol like this,
O warble forever to Northland your bliss !
And waft ye, fleet zephyrs, to every strand
This music of gladness, this joy of our land !
And, say, O ye zephyrs, who chant with the
    tide
Of Tiber, or Danube, or Severn, or Clyde,
And waves of the musical waters that pour
Enchantment to every inland and shore,
And thus have been singing through all of
    the years,
Enhancement of gladness and comfort of
    tears—
Say, zephyrs, wherever your courses ye wing,
If brighter than waters in Northland that
    sing,

If brighter ye find a wave in the world,
If lovelier the waters in Eden that purled !

II.

WHERE Mountain Monadnock, majestic
        in might
And infinite leisure, rose grand in his height,
And angels came heralds from heaven to bring
The best of May mornings to gladden the
        spring.
And waters from beechen grove sparkled
        whose wave
That charm to the hours of the bright morn-
        ing gave
Which wakens the birds to their cheeriest
        tune
And Mayfields to green to the brightness of
        June—
There, forth from the home of her humble
        life sweet,
A maiden went singing the morning to greet.
And, tranced by the resonant waters that sang

Till echoing distances joyfully rang,
She waited in wonder and awe at the song
The waters were warbling that sparkled along,
While Mountain Monadnock, rejoicing in
    might,
From foot hills to summit beamed forth his
    delight.

And rapt o'er the scene of that morning of May
The maiden entranced heard the waters to say:
" Thy motto be duty, thy jewel be truth ;
And wisdom prize ever as prizing in youth ;
And love, which to many but sorrow doth
    bring,
Shall be thy good angel to cheer thee to sing
Beyond the high music of joyfulest stream
That ever charmed poet to tunefulest theme.

"Go ask of thy mother what message I said
When hither her thoughtfulest sauntering led,
And breathing the hope of a treasure to be,
She went and months later came speaking of
    thee,

With joy and the graces of motherhood came,
Discoursing of thee and telling thy name.
Bright seasons have blossomed and blossomed
    again,
And cometh the maiden where matron came
    then.
That message, well heeded by matron, I read
In traits of the maiden, who surely will heed
The counsel, when matron shall tenderly tell
The message and ask her to honor it well."

The summers that came and the summers
    that went
To girlhood the graces of womanhood lent ;
And, lovingly loitering there by the stream,
Entranced o'er the ripple, and dimple, and
    gleam,
Two whispered the message the matron had
    told,
The words that she heard of the river of old.
And, each ripple a song and each dimple a
    gem,
The waters repeated the message to them —

That kindness of each to the other would give
To offspring best traits of each other and live
In habitudes high of childhood, to tell
Their wooing was wisdom, their mating was
     well.
Prenatal inclining to goodness, thus given !
Bestowing, ere breath, the impulse for heaven!

And later with infancy smiling they came ;
And followed another who listened to name
The father and mother breathed forth in their
     joy
And raised, at their bidding, to brow of
     the boy
Bright drops of the rivulet's musical wave,
To honor the message those waters once
     gave.
Then, looking in faith to the blue of the sky,
Each reverently prayed to the Gracious on
     high ;
And the birds and the zephyrs united in song
With voice of the waters that caroled along—
A song that was prayer for and thanks for
     the joy

Prefigured in crystal drops, there, for the boy.
And Mountain Monadnock, beholding the
  rite,
In sweetness and majesty glowed with delight.

III.

WHERE singing to mountains its reson-
  ant song
A brook from a beechen grove caroled
  along,
In chime with the robins, reflecting their
  bowers,
Inspiring the sunbeams to sweeten the flowers,
And rippling in time of the march of the
  hours
Of a morning the best that the skies could
  attune
And send from Elysium to gladden a June—
There fresh from the meads where the butter-
  cups grew,
There free as the birds from the bloom fields
  that flew,

There joyously singing child songs that he
    knew,
There charming as nature, and artless and
    true,
There bright on the morn of that June day
    of joy,
There, blithe with the breath of his blisses, a
    boy,
Impelled by the pulses prophetic of man,
In step with the waves of the rivulet ran.
Then, halting in rapture, delighted to scan
The waves of the beautiful streamlet that
    sang
Until with the carol the distances rang,
He tarried, entranced and held in high
    mood,
To muse on the song of the musical flood !

And this was the song that the rivulet sung
With its liquid lip and its silver tongue :
"In the freedom of childhood, O childhood,
    rejoice ;
Here's health to thy being and charm to thy
    voice !

The simple things love thou. as loving them
    now ;
The angels love these, and ever love thou.
Wouldst be like the eagle ? the rather the
    dove be ;
The lilies, the robins, the blue sky above thee,
Love these and be like them and angels will
    love thee,
While birds and the zephyrs shall make it
    their choice
To copy in carols the charm of thy voice.

"If wisdom be thine and if virtue attend
    thee
The blessings of heaven the Gracious shall
    send thee,
Commanding the best of His host to defend
    thee,
Bright songsters entrancing their high songs
    to sing thee,
Swift argosies gems from the far isles to
    bring thee,
And airs the rare odors of east clime to wing
    thee.

O pure as the breath of the flowers of the
    wildwood,
Forever be true to the dreams of thy child-
    hood !
And angels and good men shall ever rejoice
In the health of thy being and charm of thy
    voice."

And this was the song that the rivulet sung
With its liquid lip and its silver tongue.
And mountains responsive the cadences gave
To zephyrs that, charmed with the song of
    the wave,
The melodies far through the distances told
To angels who came with their tunefulest
    gold,
The angels who listen attentive in heaven
For singing to mortals by rivulets given.
And catching the numbers they hasten where
    gleam
The resonant waves of the musical stream,
And study its music to heighten the worth
Of songs they have learned in the land of
    their birth.

And, trying the measures in chime with the
    lay
The robins are singing in praise of the day,
They chant the blent music for cheer unto men
And soar away singing to heaven again.

Of excellent birth was the boy by the wave
That joy to the hours of the June morning
    gave.
Again there he listened, and this was the
    song
The waters were chanting that sparkled
    along :
" Who love thee will tell thee of words that I
    said
When hither good angels their sauntering led,
And tell thee, bright one of the fortunate
    birth,
What greatly shall heighten thy joy and thy
    worth
And make thy good fortune a blessing to
    earth—
A story they learned from pages they read
Till deep of its meaning their spirits had fed,

His story whose sacrifice charms away fears,
And brightens the glory of all of the years!"

"That story, ye waters, my father has told
And bade me to prize it more precious than
    gold—
The sheep and the shepherds at night on the
    plains,
The angels high chanting their heavenly
    strains,
The child in the manger, the men from afar,
And that beautiful, beautiful, wonderful
    star!"

"O pure as the breath of the flowers of the
    wildwood,
Love ever the idyl that came to thy child-
    hood!
And cherish the dreaming it gave unto thee.
For fancies of childhood, though fancies they
    be,
Have truth from that country away over sea.
Bright dreams of pure childhood, ideals from
    heaven!

The brightest of blessings that mortals are
    given !
O pure as the breath of the flowers of the
    wildwood,
Keep sacred the idyl that came to thy child-
    hood.
High born as thou art, thine heritage prize,
As steward of blessings bestowed from the
    skies.
O given from heaven that excellent worth
The instincts and temper of fortunate birth,
Not vain of thy goodness, help those who
    have less,
And be thine ambition to live but to bless.
Lift up the downfallen and lead to that One
Who knoweth how sadly some lives are begun,
Who pities their erring and knoweth each
    frame
And points from their woes to the power of
    His name."

The words of the brook to the boy by the
    wave
Awake to the wisdom its resonance gave

Were heard and remembered by angels on
    high
And chanted to sweeten the songs of the sky!
There, greeting the glad one whose June day
    of joy
Was bright with the hope and the bliss of a
    boy,
There, sweet in the dawn of some June day
    of heaven,
Shall angels enchant him with canticles given
Where singing to mountains its resonant song
A brook from a beechen grove caroled along!

PETITION.

O GOD, the griefs I cannot tell
    Give me the grace to bear,
And grant, O Lord, the faith to feel
    I have a Father's care;

The faith of patience that can wait
        Till providences prove
That things which seemed unkindest fate
        Were evidence of love ;

The faith to see Thy gracious hand
        In each untoward event,
And all 'tis hard to understand
        Believe in mercy sent ;

The faith to see through storms arise
        A waving wealth of grain,
Which, ripened by benignant skies,
        Shall all the storms explain.

O God, the griefs I may not tell
        Help me in silence bear,
And grant, O Lord, the faith to feel
        I have a Father's care.

DAY-BREAK.

AT last along the eastern sky
  The glimmerings of morn,
To end in radiance of joy
  A night of doubt and scorn !

Dread night—it was a winter long !
  And cold with winds of fate,
That still, through all their fiendish song,
  Were hot with ire of hate

And live with imps, whose interludes
  Chimed with the airs, to tell
The rancor of infernal feuds—
  Fit minstrelsy of hell !

But now the birds with carols high
  Charm all Doubt's fiends away,
And crimsons now the eastern sky,
  To hint a coming day

That shall through all its hours remain
  Unvexed by doubt and scorn,
And in the full of noon retain
  The newness of the morn !

A day whose evening shall proclaim
  That brighter dawning waits,
Fulfillment of the sunset flame,
  At the celestial gates !

BLESSINGS FOR THE HELPFUL.

GOOD friend, if every one observed
  The mandate to be kind,
If all were courteous as thyself,
  And helpfully inclined,
How bright a scene this earth would be,
  How light life's burdens prove ;
How blithe, along life's rugged road,
  Would pilgrims singing move !

The joyousness of sparkling streams
    Would bless life's desert drear ;
And birds would sing, and flowers and fruit
    With fragrance fill the air !
There is no overestimate
    Of kindness to our kind,
And brightest stars will bless the man
    To helpful ways inclined !

"O BEAUTIFUL VISION."

O BEAUTIFUL vision ! that Harmony came
And sang until Hatred and Anger grew tame,
Forgetting forever their longing for blood,
And learning of Gentleness how to be good !
And Sloth was converted and longed for
    employ,
While Envy and Slander forgot to annoy,
And toilers, contented and singing for joy,
Were glad of the hardness they had to endure,
That fitted for triumph and made it secure !

And angels were constant from heaven to
    earth
With garlands for Labor and jewels for
    Worth.
Proud Science, grown humble, endeavored to
    learn
Mechanics from insects and music from burn,
And artisans spurning their much boasted
    skill,
Saw structure in cobwebs and might in a
    rill !
Then Greed grew repentant and gave up his
    pelf,
The warrior, learning to conquer himself,
Rejoiced in the thought that at last he was
    brave,
And despots relented and ceased to enslave;
While all of the cruel, forsaking their trade,
And honest in tears for the havoc they made,
Sought only to better the world they had rent,
And proved by right living their wish to
    repent.

Yet, angel of vision, nor Harmony can,
Nor any high excellence native with man,

Ennoble mankind to the goodness like this
That breathes in thy song of the splendors of
    bliss !
Go heighten thy numbers and sing unto
    earth
The charm of His being, the glow of His
    worth,
Whose sacrifice only can give unto men
The fact of the fancy entrancing thy ken !

Thou wonderful One by the prophets
    foretold,
Thou Christ of the sages and singers of old,
O hasten the dawn of the time without tears,
The blessed, the golden, the beautiful years,
When Doubt shall be banished and all of his
    fears,
When Love from his exile shall come to his
    throne,
And Peace shall be regnant and warring
    unknown;
When men shall thirst only for waters of
    truth

And, drinking, discover the fountain of youth,
And even those destined to sin from their
    birth
Shall wake unto goodness and sing in the
    earth,
Where deserts, rejoicing, shall blossom and
    yield
Abundance to equal the long cultured field !
O hasten, Thou Gracious, the time without
    tears,
The blessed, the golden, the beautiful years,
When every one gladly shall copy Thy worth
And the splendors of bliss shall dawn on the
    earth!

CONTRAST

III.

CLARE.

A RAVEN folds his wings
  Where wild the river sings
A deep, unceasing dirge ;
And, chiming with the surge,
And sadder than the song,
The bird, the whole day long,
Cries forth from pines that sigh
Beneath November's sky !
Yet vain the chant, how vain
The whole commingled strain,
To give a full relief,
Or even lessen grief,
When over loved ones slain,
Bereavéd hearts complain
That woman false should prove
To constancy of love.
In vain the pine trees sigh,
And bird and river try
To tell their blessings fled
Who mourn their Roderick dead.
For he such joy had given,
To them he seemed from heaven.

But came a fateful day
To sweep their hopes away !
Protecting angels ! spare
The earth from more like Clare,
Who lit, to quench, the fires
Of love's supreme desires,
Joyed o'er the fading glow,
Laid then the altar low,
And gloried in the guilt
To wreck the temple built
Of peace, by hope, above
The silver shrine of love.
And these in ruin say
How sad that fateful day.
Betrothed from her own choice,
To make his heart rejoice
Who faithfully and well
Had loved, by message fell
Clare put his joy to rout
And ruthless blotted out
The star that makes men glad
And, failing, drives them mad.

At middle of the night,
When hope had borne such blight

'Twere midnight were it noon,
November were it June !
Doubt's night, when 'gainst despair,
Worst fiend of all that are,
The lover long had striven,
At midnight, demon-driven —
He knew not what he did !
Blame him ?   O Heaven forbid !
And Heaven their hearts sustain
Who mourn their Roderick slain.
And yet they bravely keep
Life's course while still they weep.
And braver than to live,
The sorrowing ones forgive
The cruelty of art
That broke a lover's heart
And drove him to the deed
For which their hearts must bleed
Throughout the desert years,
And they shed bitter tears
O'er one with sweetest worth
That ever perfumed earth,
O'er one whom traitor gave
To an untimely grave.

So of this sadness voiceful surge
Of river sang, and so the dirge
Of pines, and all the winds that blew,
Told what no yeoman was but knew,
No dullest vision but could see
Was useless here more witchery.
Yet here, where seem the rocks in tears
And giant oaks to thrill with fears,
The artful Clare dissembles pain
Of grieving love o'er lover slain,
Till some repenting scorn they gave,
Of feigning Clare her pardon crave,
And speak in tones that fall like rain
On thirsty herbs of fevered plain !
The hint of wish to fare away
They gently chide, and press to stay,
And beg a frequent friendly word
By postman fleet or carrier bird.
Then, flushing fine from their caress
Who pray celestial graciousness
The grief-rent heart of Clare to bless,
The queen of arts that did not fail
Goes forth to quest in other vale !

How many there her arts reward
The song were weighted to record.

Yet many 'twas, and there, of all
Entranced, but one too brave to fall.
This Donald was, blithe, wise and strong,
From land of heather and of song—
So gallant, unobtrusive, good,
'Twere naught to read the noble blood
Descended from some hardy clan
Whose valor back to Wallace ran,
And blended, in the days of eld,
With might the glorious Bruces held.
Discerning Scot, as Scots are born,
With inner sight to ken and warn,
He read her arts and read to scorn,
Aud tossed a calm, derisive " nay,"
And said, as needless 'twere to say,
" Fair one, withhold the huntsman's horn,
Nor urge thy steed the chase forlorn.
Although thine arrows oft have slain,
To speed them here again were vain,
Till easier game thine eyes shall see
Before thee, queen of archery ! "

Defeated once, but hopeful still,
The artful is victorious till,

Returning where her course begun,
Art wins again where erst it won.
Inbreathing, from the airs that fleet
And from the souls her arts defeat,
New qualities of woman's power
To add to her abundant dower,
Audacious grows the conquering Clare,
Till, daring sacred precincts where
The ashes loved of Roderick sleep,
And bowed bereavement comes to weep,
She startles from affection's prayer
The kin and comrades faithful there—
Yet artful so they near believe
Her artfulness, that would deceive
Almost the angels of the skies,
So saintly seem her sophistries !
Assuming role of mourner, too,
Who sorrows more than others do,
She comes in tears and tearful goes,
Returns in tears and plants a rose,
And tarries oft in practice there,
To learn the art to feign a prayer ?

Thus once from dawn to evening star,
When stranger fared who came from far,

From England's coast, in quest of fame,
From England's coast, with Albion's
    name.
Though great his English consequence
And all sufficient for defence
Against most pleasures aimed to try
To swerve from his endeavors high,
It was not proof against the Clare
Discovered thus by Albion there,
A lovely grief alone at prayer!

If power there be in woman's smiles,
How thrice bewitching are the wiles
Of woman tremulous with fears,
Of woman grieving unto tears.
And charming if the grief sincere,
Her sorrow feigned more cause for fear,
When greater than the true appear
The acted sigh, and look, and tear.

Tell not the story, though 'tis brief,
Of Albion won by woman's grief,

So fully won that those who warned
He heeded not till charmer scorned.
Tell not the tale, though briefly said,
Of Albion loving, Albion dead,
Self-slain because refused by Clare,
The charming grief he found at prayer.
How great the woes of woman due
At Roderick's grave and Albion's, too!
At hint of day she weeps by one,
By other with the setting sun!
But yonder, poised on buoyant wings,
An angel messenger, who sings :
" Fair one and false, inconstant Clare,
'Twere ill for one from upper air
For once a woman's mind to taint
With words that any vices paint
To which her cruelties have driven
Good men whose virtues, sweet to heaven,
Bloomed fragrant on the airs of earth
With odors of celestial worth !
And who shall tell the griefs that crazed
Till calmest minds erratic blazed,
Then sank forever in the night
Of deepest hopelessness of blight !
Or who describe the crimson tide
Where love, defeated, rashly died !

Although the busy following years
Of triumphs won through causing tears,
May for the moment thrust aside
Remembrance of the first who died
To whom, in plighting troth, she lied,
Not long doth Clare forget, I ween,
The color of the tragic scene
When he went out a darkened way.
Not even Clare forgets that day —
Not even Clare, where'er she stray.
Not even Clare doth long forget
The sadness of the sun that set
When first a victim of her slight
Rushed, wild despairing, into night!

"But that dark night shall have a morn,
O Clare, who didst his pleading scorn,
A morn when thou from night shall see
His spirit in felicity,
High mated in that country where
No one like thee shall ever dare,
O fair, inconstant, cruel Clare!

" Forgiven by his gracious kin
Thy keenest cruelty of sin,

Straight from his death, all unoppressed,
Thou faredst forth on other quest,
To win again, again to prove
Thy sure inconstancy of love.
And now, although in pride arrayed
And flushing from achievements made,
Thou comest to dissemble here
The power to shed a truthful tear,
And try the feat of feigning, Clare,
The awe and agony of prayer,
To aid thee sorrowing love to feign,
That should another lover gain
For thee to crush, to see his pain !
Then thou wouldst drink his being up
And toss aside the broken cup
That was a faithful lover's self,
As but the pence of beggar's pelf,
And forth to other conquest fare,
Inconstant and insatiate Clare !
Responsive to thy nature's call,
Here Albion gave to thee his all.
Drank thou his soul to thy delight,
And all his power, to give thee might.
Drank thou with that high ecstasy
That speaks a woman's liberty ;
And then, the consummation done,

Thou, cruel, fair, inconstant one,
With might he gave didst giver slay,
And say to all his pleadings nay—
Thy victor soul to steel didst turn
And Albion from thy presence spurn ;
And alternated back to prayer,
Still other souls to charm and snare !
Nor wouldst thou rest until thine arts
Had snared and drunk a thousand hearts,
That each increased the art of Clare
By thousand fold of power to snare,
And all the kingliest of the earth,
Mistaking artfulness for worth,
Should rave in eloquence of praise
Of thine enrapturing ways,
Or cringe, meek suppliants for thy smiles,
And, for them rivals by thy wiles,
Should die in duels for thine hand
Till rashness reddened every land !
With airs to sigh a deep refrain
And stars in tears above the slain
That cumbered every plain
From northmost to Antarctic main,
And mighty angels trembling o'er
The prodigality of gore
From Orient to western shore,

And saints, forgetting bliss on high,
To shudder with the peaceful sky—
This, this, O Clare, were unto thee
The acme of felicity !

"But thou shalt never capture more,
Thy day of conquest now is o'er !
'Tis mine, fair one, the word to speak
That, spoken, must life's tenure break.
To some that word is but a boon ;
Yet unto most it comes too soon.
But seem it soon, or seem it late,
Or mean it boon, or mean it fate,
Or seem it just, or seem it fell,
When missioned here, that word I tell ;
For I, fair one, am Azrael.
And here that word as dart I send
Thine artful cruelty to end !"

The listener speechless, quivering stood,
Then, reeling, staggered toward the flood.
The spurning waves soon cast ashore,
And fishers, finding, pitying bore

To lonely glen and buried there,
Where meagre marble reads of Clare !
There weird the pensive pine trees sigh
Beneath the gray November sky,
And raven comes on sombre wings
And gruesome to the river sings,
That, chanting sad and ceaseless strain,
Bears burden to the distant main
Of love that perfidy hath slain.
And, mournful whispering with the dirge,
Distinct above the river's surge,
And sigh of pine and note of bird,
The spirit of a voice is heard :
" *O maiden fair, do thou be true,*
Or thou shalt long thy falseness rue !
O woman false, beware, beware !
Repent thy ways, give heed to Clare ! "

O who shall tell the damning guilt
Of her who wrecks ideal built—
By her desired, by her inspired—
By lover by her wishes fired.
Than this there is no greater crime
In all the rounds of troubled time,
Beneath the wide-beholding sun—
Who murders love, hath murder done !

INTERLUDE.

O ye compelled to be
Acquaint with perfidy
Till ye might think that Clare
Was type of all the fair,
Come where the roses rare,
And clover blooming there,
Shed forth upon the air
The story of a love
Whose fragrance cheers above
The breath of sweetest June
Of Summer's boon !

LILLIAN.

Where sweet a shining river
    Flows singing to the sea
And purls with charming cadence
    Where smiling landscapes be,
Gemmed bright with pleasant mansions,
    That in perspective seem

The counterpart of castles
　　That fill youth's brightest dream—
There, sweet within the valley,
　　In other days a scene
That fills with choicest fragrance
　　The years that intervene !

And for that scene the valley
　　A finer verdure spreads
When, cheering after winter,
　　The May sun radiance sheds.
And brighter flame and crimson
　　And lovelier dun and gold
The hardy mountain beeches
　　And valley maples hold,
When frost and autumn sunshine
　　Their chemistry have done,
In glorious completion
　　Of work the spring begun.

Dear vale of Metawampe !
　　Sweet by the sunrise shore

Of thy majestic river,
  Delightful evermore,
An arbor was where Lillian,
  Who Leon promise made
But later wrecked the plighting,
  By unwise kindred swayed,
Returned, at last, repentant,
  To bid his hope relive,
And there so bravely humble,
  Knelt asking him forgive.

And quick above the sadness
  That darkened weary years
And weighted him with sorrow
  Exceeding words and tears,
There broke serenest radiance
  That ever augured day,
Or woke a heart to courage,
  Or lit a wanderer's way.

  With gentle hand,
  In fairyland,
To thoughts sublime she led him';

With grandest views,
And nectar dews,
And heavenly fruitage, fed him ;
From field and sky
And mountain high,
Inspiring lessons read him ;
With tender art,
From her true heart,
A sincere promise said him,
Naming a day,
A month away,
A happy day to wed him.

That good day came
With sweetest flame
The Orient ever lighted,
To signalize
The golden ties
Of loving hearts united !
Day sweet with airs
That banished cares
And to high thoughts incited ;
Day spanned with blue,
The whole day through !

As if all wrongs were righted
And sang the lark
Till all birds dark
Had flown from earth affrighted !

The honeymoon
Could not end soon
Of two so nobly mated,
But still would shine
Were skies benign,
Or if to grief storms fated.

Their love kept new,
For each soul grew ;
And each the other aided
Right things to know
To help each grow,
And love's rose never faded !

Sweet vale of Metawampe !
Therein, since that dear day,

Auspicious time for trysting
    The silver nights of May.
For, then, from favoring Heaven,
    Swift where the lovers wait,
Thrilled with the thoughts surpassing
    All else however great,

Fly ministrants commissioned
    To utter words that save
From cowardice the lover
    And make the maiden brave.
And when the pledge is spoken
    To crown love's high emprise,
They soar from Metawampe,
    To tell the waiting skies !

IDYLS OF FREEDOM

IV.

THE GREAT SACRIFICE.

O STARS, what history
    It has been yours to see
Enacted here, since man,
Crown of creation's plan,
His wanderings began—
Since to his pristine joy
He added an alloy
That forth a rover sent
Him, fired with discontent.
Say since, with Eden lost,
The fateful bounds he crossed,
How dear his straying cost !
Still, while in wretched plight,
He was not hopeless quite,
Nor rayless was his night.

Stars that have kindly shone
On paths his feet have gone—
Than downward, let us hope,
Onward more, and up—

Aid still his wish and quest
For truth, and peace and rest.
Still from the blue above
Shine where he wars to prove
His patriotic love,
And, dying, asks you tell
The ages that he fell
To foil the tyrant's hand
And bless his native land.
And tell, as tell ye must,
O stars, for stars are just,
From what great sacrifice
All others do arise.
Tell what, foreseen, inspired,
And what, accomplished, fired,
The patriotic heart to live
For liberty and give
His life to make men free.
And aid, O stars, to see
That highest liberty.
Gives equal weight of care,
Gives unto each his share
Of burdens all must bear ;
That liberty, if boon,
Used wrongly, cometh soon
To license, that is not

True liberty, but blot
On the historic page,
A hindrance to the age.

This life, this sacrifice,
O stars, from which arise
The heavenly blessings given
And hope of more in heaven—
This life of hope for man,
Ye saw as it began.
Ye saw its teeming day,
O stars, and sunset ray,
And deathly chill of night,
And hint at last of light.
Ye saw the glorious morn
Of grace and peace adorn
The mountain heights of time
And shine to every clime,
To make all life sublime !
A star 'twas guided them
Who fared to Bethlehem ;
And at cerulean poise
It sentineled their joys,
As o'er the Savior born,

Rejoicing till the morn,
They mused on what should be
His wondrous history.
Stars gave the warning dream
Of Herod's hellish scheme
And guided, then, the flight
To Egypt through the night.
And o'er the child returned
The stars in gladness burned.

The stars rejoiced the boy
And study gave and joy,
As through the years he grew
To all the ages knew—
Till wondering sages gazed
Adoring and amazed.
Stars cheered the Christ who prayed
In lonely mountain glade,
And sang their joy to see
The helpful ministry
Of Him of Galilee.
And when his followers slept
Ye stars in pity wept ;
And, weeping, wondered ye

At the sublimity
Of sad Gethsemane !
And when at Calvary
The sun refused to shine,
Your stellar beams were sign
That Christ, the slain, should rise,
Completed sacrifice,
Triumphant to the skies !

Ye stars that wondering saw
His answer to the law
Who for the sinful died
And poured the precious tide
Of His great life, to give
The sinful chance to live—
Ye stars who heard the word
Sublimest ever heard,
That Jesus at His death
Spoke with His dying breath,
To say the work was done,
The victory was won —
From that sublimity,
That matchless agony,
All greatness doth proceed.

Thence every noble deed,
Thence all unselfishness,
Thence every pulse to bless
That helps the patriot die,
Without the question why,
For home and liberty.

AMERICA.

ON days and deeds sublime
  That gem this western clime,
O stars of Freedom, shine,
And shed your beams benign
Where Concord bridge was won,
And rustic Lexington—
And Bunker Hill declared,
And Bennington, how fared
The foes of liberty
Who warred against the free.

Shine where the great and good
With high solicitude,

In meekness knelt to pray
To Heaven to drive away
The foreign foes and give
The country chance to live.
How humble and how great,
How fit to found a state,
Was he who knelt that day,
At Valley Forge, to pray !
And may his land remain
The place of all good gain
And Freedom's own domain,
The home and resting place
Of bravery and of grace,
Of greatness and all worth—
The paradise of earth !

Though truth the charm will break,
Still best the truth to speak.
Here, where 'twas general boast
That this was Freedom's coast,
Were human beings chained,
While Selfishness explained
That slavery was right.
And those who saw the plight
That Liberty was in,

By league with such a sin,
And dared rebuke the wrong,
That still was growing strong,
While grew the nation weak
To danger that 'twould break,
Were stigmatized as fools
Beyond discretion's rules.
But in these later days,
The scoffers dare the praise
That radicals were wise
And fit to canonize
For the sublimest skies !

How cursed this sin the land
We came to understand
When Donelson was need
And Fredericksburg, and greed
Of rough-hewn havoc made
On Sherman's master raid
Of horse and infantry
From inland to the sea !
And need to prove our liege
To liberty was siege
Of Vicksburg and the shock
Of "Chickamauga's Rock,"

Grim Thomas of the build
To name for Cæsar's guild.
So Grierson's reckless dash,
Discreet in that 'twas rash ;
And Farragut in the shrouds,
And Hooker in the clouds,
And Ellsworth first to die,
And gallant Lyon—why
So early sent to heaven !
And why McPherson given,
And thousands, thousands more !
How runneth up the score,
Through scenes of din and gore,
To Gettysburg, sublime
Through all the years of time !

What tongue can tell, what pen,
The fate of prisoned men
Who, doomed to the ill
Of Andersonville,
Learned the tortures that spell
A new name for hell !
And who can count their tears
And warring hopes and fears,
Who mourned their loved ones there,

Or slain in conflict, where,
Though glorious thus to fall
For country and for all
That's dear, and true, and high,
'Twas fearful, still, to die !
And hard was it to know
That with the slaughter, slow
Moved the cause of right
And darkened down the night
Of doubt, with scarce a ray
To hint of coming day.
But rose a lustrous star
When he led on the war
Whose calm, courageous way
Of hero in affray,
Assured, at once, a morn,
And was the sign to warn
The foemen of defeat
Their cause was sure to meet.

Now once and three times three,
At Appomattox tree,
Give every one to all
Who heeded Freedom's call
And marched with Grant, to hew

The hard-fought journey through
The Wilderness, to see
The dawn of victory.

But who shall sing to tell
Their deeds who fought and fell
In all the hard campaigns,
Who equal epic strains
For those whose crimson stains
Full thrice a hundred plains,
And reddens bloody years,
Which make them high compeers
Of all the brave that Time
Hath brought to wreath and rhyme!

Let gratitude be given
In joyful song to Heaven ;
Aye, shout and sing again,
Good citizens, that when
The nation was in dole
A man of prophet soul
Was sent to meet our need.

A man inspired to read
The meaning of the times
The country for its crimes
Was going through,—this man,
With genius fit to plan
And brave enough to act,
Made thus his vision fact,
Wielding the nation's might
For mercy and the right,
And breaking. at a stroke,
The bondman's galling yoke.

Good stars, your radiance shed
On paths where Lincoln led
Through all those years of strife
Up to the higher life
Of Freedom and of peace
And all the good increase
That makes these states combined
The envy of mankind !

IN OTHER LANDS.

GOOD stars, what prophet ken
    Had Aztec Juarez, when
For liberty he fought
Against the foe who sought
To bind with Spanish chain
The Mexican in train
Of papal Rome, to slave
Subservient where the brave
Descendants of the sun
Their long career had run,
Free as the airs that fanned
Their lovely native land.
Well ye rejoiced, to see
Where foreign tyranny
Had reigned, superior rise,
To crown the high emprise
Of Juarez with success
And so mankind to bless,
The fair republic bright
With promise for the right
Of patriots everywhere.
For each hath right to share
Each country of the free,
Wherever dwelleth he.

Still Juarez only did
As high examples bid—
Through thirty years of blood,
When that brave Swede withstood
The papal powers combined,
Who sought on all mankind
To place the Latin yoke—
Gustavus brave, who broke
The bondage long and sore
For northmen evermore.
He drove the power of Rome
From church, and court, and home,
Wherein the people sing,
To crown Gustavus king !
And cadence of the song
The southland doth prolong,
Where well Emmanuel strove
And Garibaldi's love
Was given for Italy,
Mankind and liberty.

And Magyars, whose Kossuth
For country and for truth
Was sacrifice, may raise
To favoring Heaven their praise

For his grand life, and twine
The wreath and pray the Nine
To sing to full import
That high in Austrian court
The Magyars reign, whom erst
The tyrant Austrians cursed !

How bright the stars that look
On Scotland's famous brook
And bid the ages learn
That Bruce of Bannockburn
Was Caledonia's pride !
Shine where her sons defied,
At Flodden field, the foe
That laid her banner low,
Yet in defeat were strong
To height of grandest song.
Beam kind on every glen
Known to his foot and ken,
That kingliest of men,
The Wallace of the Eld,
Whom, then, ye stars beheld
And sang him worthy praise
Of all the future days.

Shine, stars, with beams benign
On scene of deeds divine,
Where Winkelried the brave,
His Switzerland to save,
Threw on the Austrian steel
His mighty rage of zeal
And struck in death the blow
To break the serried foe.
His followers, raining blows
Where grand his courage rose,
Thus turned the tide and day
Against the cruel fray
Of those who sought t' enslave
The Switzer patriots brave,
Whom God's own mountains gave
That love of liberty
That fits men to be free.

And evermore shall ye,
Bright stars of liberty,
Rejoice to shine upon
The field where Cromwell won,
At Marston Moor, the day
And stemmed the tyrant's sway,

Till full at Naseby, then,
Where royal Charles again
Marshaled his hosts, the band
Of patriots dared withstand
The legions of the king ;
And all the years shall sing,
To let the future know,
They routed him to show
That foreign he, and foe,
Though native born—for he
Loved not true liberty.

The truth alone gives rate,
The citizen's estate,
A country and a place,
Fraternity and race.
Alien to truth, a man
Nor country hath, nor clan,
Though castled well and crowned
With choicest treasures found
In late or olden times,
Through west or Orient climes.
Aye, foreign he, and poor,
And sick, though mount and moor

Afford their gold for wealth
And myrrhs to bless his health.
Not loving truth, then he
Shall poor and homeless be,
Though heraldry declare
That ancient lineage rare
Makes him the rightful heir
To every land and throne,
And though the people own
The purple of his power,
Rejoicing in his dower
And seeking bards to sing
Him bishop, lord and king !
But rhyme they ne'er so well,
The bards who seek to tell
An untruth in a song
And sing success of wrong—
Some Crœsus toast for wealth
That came alone by stealth,
And hymn the tyrant's might
As given by heavenly right—
Will sing but meagre praise.
And, faltering in the lays
Whose labored lines confess
They sing from selfishness,

They'll rave to furious stress
Of prayer to Power to bless,
When Truth alone gives theme
Befitting poet's dream.

Yet strange contrasts arise,
Some royal mysteries—
A king to virtue known,
Yet who could make his throne,
By tricks that must belong
The hellish arts among,
The anchor of a wrong
That should have scourge of'song,
The very rage of rhyme,
To blast to future time !
The Charles whom Cromwell fought,
True to his home, was naught
But false to native land
Though promising, his hand
Withheld the needed good
He pledged to those who stood
For liberty and right.
For these did Cromwell fight ;
For these he overthrew

The Stuart king and slew
The false one of the throne.
And by the act was shown
In England evermore—
A truth the wide world o'er,
And as the sunlight plain—
The right of kings to reign,
Original in heaven,
Is to the governed given,
By them to be transferred,
In their installing word,
To those their love shall say
The kingly traits display.
Would Cromwell had remained,
Preventing crime that stained
Bright Albion's sovran name,
By other Charles who came,
The Charles who ever wrought
Injustice and who thought
Of self alone, and sought
Delight in splendid sin
And seemed possessed to win,
By elegance of shame,
An ever florid fame
Unto his royal name !

ARRAIGNMENT OF RUSSIA.

IF ill the theme befits
   To sirg of Austerlitz,
If vain to weep a while
By lone Helena's isle,
If cold, to some, such theme
For patriotic dream,
In that the Corsican
Fought not for fellow-man,
But strove alone for fame
For his imperial name—
O would some one as rod
Of an avenging God,
Arise, who, sent by wrath
Of Heaven, should cleave a path
Through Tyranny's domains
To far Siberia's plains,
And break the prison bars
Of victims of the czars !

The cause demands a man
Serener, grander than

The dreaded Corsican?
May one with like strong hand
And genius to command,
Arise—some leader born
Under the star of morn,
Some one whose shining worth
Shall win the best of earth
To highest hope and prayer
For Heaven's especial care,
And win good gallant men
To join his flag, whose ken
At once, from far, can see
The day of victory—
The men with might to win
The boon their faith hath seen.

O, chieftain of the skies!
And Freedom's cause, arise,
And, panoplied for wars,
Go guided by the stars
That favoring shone
Above Napoleon,
In that sublime advance
From his admiring France

That made the Russias quake
And all the kingdoms shake !
Stars, they, to aid to see
The way to victory ;
Stars that would lustrous burn,
To light the grand return
Of victors from the fray
Where justice won the day.

Not so the march when Ney
Fared on the frozen way,
To cheer his leader back
Along the winter track,
With remnant of his host,
To mourn the prize they lost,
A city burned to ban
The mighty Corsican.
Him Russia dared not fight,
But put to sorry plight
By burning roof and bread
That should have housed and fed
The host, who froze or starved
By thousands ere they carved,
With Bonaparte and Ney

To France their pilgrim way.
But those engaged
In warring waged
To break the dungeon bars
Of prisoned worth, ye stars
Would good birds send to feed,
Unto their fullest need,
With manna of the Heaven
That bread hath ever given
To those who well have striven,
Through hard or favored fight,
In furtherance of right.

If Moscow burned again
'Twould light the prisoned men
From durance hard to flee
To hope and liberty,
The men whose dungeon bars
Are legacy of czars,
Kings whose oppression is
Acme of tyrannies !
Commanding those away
In bondage sore to stay,
Whose glances have told,

Or a breath over bold,
That the fancies they hold
Slight hindrances are
To the wish of a czar !
Dooming banishment
For the mildest intent
Of the patriot heart !
O tyrant ! what art
Of what spirit malign
Of the demons is thine !
How strange that czars should ban
Those whom but easy plan
Of right would lead to own
Allegiance to the throne
And give their life to prove
Their loyalty of love
And interest in the fame
Of Alexander's name !
But heeding not the cries
That move the pitying skies
And make the nations weep,
These Tartar tyrants keep
Their hand of tyranny
Against all liberty.

O, when Sarmatia's brave
With Kosciusko gave

Most valorous blows to save
Their country from the grave
That fierce tyrannic might
Had dug for Truth and Right,
Say, Heaven of justice, say,
Why did Thy vengeance stay
From smiting down her foes !
O! when to Thee arose
Their patriotic cry,
Why, Heaven of pity, why
Should fail thy mighty arm
To shield their land from harm !

And fell Sarmatia, then !
And her heroic men,
Whose patriotic worth
Had brightened all the earth,
Were graced with exiles' chains
And scourged across the plains
Afar to foreign strand,
And there were given brand
Befitting felon band ;
Aye, there were given rate
Meaner than murderer's fate,

Whose hands the blood had spilt
Of parricidal guilt !
Yet, there, the scorn of slaves,
Do these Sarmatian braves
Display, despite the gloom
Of their Siberian doom,
The rare sweet quality
Of fitness to be free !

Stay, Angel of the Book
Of Record, stay, and look !
For this is far from all
Of Poland's direful thrall
From Russia's might, whose whole
Of tyrant dirt and dole
Hath hue of Herod's crime,
And seems of Nero's time !
Fair women sent to pine
In dark and noisome mine !
Or sent with felon's chain
To walk the weary plain
Where mercy hath no rate,
Where hunger hath no sate

But cup and crust of hate !
Or hath she darker fate
That is so worse than death
It is not given breath !

Nor is this all, for there,
Condemned to exile's fare,
The patriot's children know
Maturity of woe !
O angel ! and ye stars !
Enduring still the czars !
What Herod edict this !
Ukase to blot the bliss
From childhood's heart of joy,
That never knew alloy
Of ill, nor thought to stray
In sin's forbidden way,
And so most rightfully
The heir of liberty,
Entitled to be free
As nature's minstrelsy
Of zephyrs, birds, and rills
That sing to freedom's hills !

Read not the story through,
Read not of Finn or Jew,
Read not, though each have felt
The blows the tyrants dealt
To emphasize their hate
Of freedom's good estate.
Enough the monster crime
That chilled Sarmatia's clime,
Enough what Poland braved
Ere Russian hate enslaved,
Enough the robber rout
That blotted Poland out !
Enough is one page
Of Tyranny's rage !
Enough is the brief
Of exiles in grief !

O ye who are given,
As natives of heaven,
The quality high
Of grace of the sky,
That maketh secure
Where none could endure
Devoid of the dower
Of heavenly power,

Could even the might
Of sons of the light
Fit an angel to bear,
If, gifted so rare,
An angel should dare,
To con the dread score
Of pillage and gore
That causes the wail
From Vistula's vale !
Or ponder the woes
The banished one knows
In Tyranny's chains
On far away plains !

O ! the desolate strand
Where Hate turns the land
Into barrenest sand !
While Doubt freezes there
Till even the air
Is chill with despair
And dread as the breath
Of the spectre of death !

In spite of the chill
That freezes to kill,
There facile ones fly

From nethermost sky,
Who, artful in eye
And skillful to lie,
From seeming at first
On mission accurst
From regions the worst,
Soon look to repent
Of evil intent,
And, merciful bent,
From sinister gleams
Quick vary to beams
Of a twinkling that seems
The hopefulest ray
Of the splendors of day !
And the lustre that glints
Deceives as the hints
That rosiest morn
The waste shall adorn,
Where no morning can come
To the castaway's gloom !

There swift from below,
There joyful at woe,
There charmed with a moan,

There rapt o'er a groan,
There others have flown,
Who missioned of Night,
Who buoyant at blight,
Who sportive at chains
Harsh clanking o'er plains
Where Tyranny reigns,
Sing gleeful at cries
Of anguish that rise
From the victims of hate
In the bondage of fate,
Begirt with their dead
And trembling with dread
Of still deeper gloom
To darken their doom !
But have harpers of hell
The numbers to tell
The gloom of a cell
Of Saghalien, where dwell
The good and the brave
Whom tyrants enslave,
Or the murk of the mines
Where hope never shines,
No, never, through years
Of the saltest of tears !

Read not the story through ;
One page alone will do !
One page alone of dread,
One page with terror red,
One page of hot tears shed,
One page of that despair
Which fades the eye and hair
Saps e'en the power to cry,
Gives a hot thirst to die,
Kills the smile on the face,
Blots the last look of grace,
Blots the last mental trace,
Stills the hand from device,
Chills the blood into ice,
And the nerves into bone,
And the heart into stone !

O what chieftain would dare
In the lists with despair,
Though grandly he fare
From tournaments where
The giants, aflame
With the passion for fame,
Contend in the fray
Of chivalry's day !
Aye, came he away

Unhewn and complete
And longing to meet
Far fiercer than those
He found to oppose,
What victor would dare
To cope with despair ?
How dead the heart, how dead,
With hope forever fled !
And yet 'tis so quick
That it trembles at tick
Of the seconds of time
And the pulsing of rhyme
Of the song that keeps tune
With the cadence of June !
Though despairing till dead,
Yet it trembles with dread
At the tenderest song
That is wafted along
Over clover and corn
On the breath of the morn !
And it quivers and quakes
At a zephyr that shakes
But as gently as jar
Of the beams of a star
That in rose-scented hours,
Bright glancing in bowers,

Responds to the flowers
That smile, to invite
The cheer of the light
Of the beauty of heaven,
In stellar beams given.

Aye, there's never a heart
That's alive to all art
And is beating in chime
With nature's sweet rhyme
But if conquered by fear
Would shudder to hear
Even music of waves
Of the streamlet that laves
The myrtle banks sweet
Where fairy ones meet,
In elfin land grove,
To warble of love !
Aye, held by despair,
No victim could bear
Breath from elfin land, where
But a breath of the air
Of the earth would displace
The planets that trace

Round the fairy land sun
The courses they run.
What then is the fate
Of the victims of hate
Of the despot who reigns
O'er the Russian domains,
And his victims doth cast
To the pitiless blast
Of northland, or wills
That in Caucasus hills
They shall dig till they die,
And dishonored shall lie
In a far away grave
Too mean for a slave !

O Heaven ! whose lurid star
Maddens to might and war,
When thou shalt undertake
The Russian yoke to break,
Say, Heaven of justice, say,
What blood can ever pay
The wrong to Poland done
By those whose ravage won
By Vistula's fair tide,
That, often crimson-dyed
From noblest patriot slain,
Goes moaning to the main !

Ye thrice ten thousand dead,
Whose blood the Cossacks shed
In homes of Praga fair,
How eloquent your prayer—
A plea to Heaven to aid
A land in ruin laid !
And emphasis of gore
Hath this from thousands more
Where Warsaw's reddened plains,
That Freedom's ichor stains,
And Cracow's crimsoned sod,
Still wail their plaints to God !
Fair Wanda's mountain moans,
Responsive to the groans,
And Dnieper makes her cry,
For Dniester to reply ;
And from the Don to San,
Rebuking Russian ban,
Blood red the waters gleam
Of each Sarmatian stream !
Whichever way it track,
To Baltic or the Black,
Sad, sad each river flows,
A requiem of woes,
From Poland to the seas,
That chant her miseries !

VISION AND PROPHECY.

ON Ural hils it came,
    A tongue of prophet flame,
A burning thither sent
From out the firmament
Of justice, love and truth,
And everlasting youth.
And thus the fervid voice :
"O tyrant ! have thy choice
To turn to righteousness
And teach thy hands to bless—
Repent the despot's crime,
Worst cruelty of time,
Or take the doom that falls
Thereon—the mighty walls
Of tyranny thrown down,
The dimmed and wrested crown
Of monarchs in defeat,
With conscience to repeat
To all the winds that fleet—
' The tyrant's fate is meet ! ' "
Thus, while the bright night heard,
Swift flew the warning word
And sought by westward star

The palace of the czar.
There, round the festive board,
His nobles and their lord
Glowed o'er their ruddy wine,
In toast of new design
To make the exiles weep
And keep the world asleep.

But. stay, why trembles he?
What vision doth he see ?
No ghost in festive hall,
No hand upon the wall,
To make his pleasures pall.
No fiend his eyes detect ;
No peasant to suspect.
Tried ministers attend,
Full foot and horse defend
The throne and citadel
Where czar and kindred dwell,
And, cordonned round the land,
Grim guarding legions stand !
Yet pales the czar with dread !
He thinks assassins tread,

With blade athirst and blast,
To drink his blood and cast,
In atoms to the sky,
The halls of tyranny !

The voice from Ural hills
Flamed forth hath gone in thrills
Of swiftest breezes blown
Along the northern zone,
And many leagues afar
In palace of the czar
With trembling terror fills,
To consternation chills,
The ruler of the land.
And not invention planned
To keep supreme at home
His reign, if foes should come,—
And not ambitious schemes
That give him pleasant dreams
Of other lands to gain,
Of widening domain
To great increase of dower,
To boundlessness of power—
Not one of these, nor all,

Can break the chilling thrall,
And drive the fiends away
That on his spirit prey !

And evermore shall cling
Those fiends, and tear and sting,
And for new vigor drink
The ichor, black as ink,
Of veins of tyranny
That fed on liberty
Through many, many years,
Drank river floods of tears
And jeered a thousand sneers
At patriotic sighs
Drawn by a czar's emprise !

After the burning spoke
And round the echoes woke,
Responsive to the doom
The flame announced to come,—
Soft blazed the voice of truth,
In tones of tender ruth
Of love's sweet firmament,
A message eastward sent

By one appearing there
From out the upper air,
Who seemed to high emprise
Commissioned by the skies,
He wore that loveliness
That doth high worth express
In angel or in men
Of angel mien and ken.

Away on zephyrs borne,
He came at tinge of morn
To bleak Siberian strand,
The northern demonland!
There imps abound in air
Who give their constant care
That when the tyrants die
Some sprite of ill shall fly
To convoy them to hell,
Reporting there how well
They have performed the work
The monarch of the murk
Assigns, and thus, how far
They have obeyed the czar.
From spirit of the sky
The imps affrighted fly.

And well escaped his might,
They pause them in their flight
And hiss, in powerless ire,
Their breath of spiteful fire,
That freezes on the air.
And now they backward fare,
To see if stranger sprite
Shall think him to alight.
And soon he turns to fly,
That bright one of the sky,
His plumage to begrime,
Down through the jagged rime
Of rock where guardsmen pace,
To keep the exile race.
And this the word of cheer
The toilers, listening hear :
" Good patience, still, ye braves
Condemned to fate of slaves !
Against Oppression's throne,
The Mighty makes His own
The cause of those who, long
In suffering, still are strong."
Glad on his herald tongue
The delvers hopeful hung.
Yet scarce could angel's cheer
Dispel an exile's fear.

Forth then the voice of flame ;
And soon a lovelier came—
An angel with this word :
" The message ye have heard
Was told to me in heaven,
Whence all good gifts are given.
So strange 'twas thought 'twould seem,
So fanciful the dream,
Another one was sent
Attesting the intent
Of powers above to bless
With buoyance in duress
And exodus from chains
To Freedom's own domains."

The angel ceased and drew
A stylus forth of hue
Of the cerulean blue
And ruby stone and white,
And straight began to write
Upon the prison mine
With deep cut lustrous sign.
No words the delving said,
But breathless watched and read ;
And forth the angel fled.

Came then a third to say :
" Toilers, ye have seen to-day
Two of the seven prized most
Of the selectest host
Of all the armies bright
Bannered in realms of light.
Aflame with brightest star,
That host ten thousand are,
With place of honor given
The thousand best of heaven,
They who the most have blessed,
As heaven's accounts attest,
The sorrowing ones of earth,
And honored most true worth.
And those a hundred best
Have placed before the rest,
The hundred giving seven
Most pleasing unto Heaven
The highest, foremost place
Of all the angel race.
" And, of this number, one
Is Uriel of the sun.
And Raphael gracious is
And given to ministries,
And most sublimities

Hath missioned been to see,
And most of misery.
The first your boon to tell
Was flaming Uriel,
And Raphael who came
To witness Uriel's flame
And cheer with face benign
The delvers in this mine.

"Led Israfil the throng
In that first Christmas song
That told the waiting earth
Of a Redeemer's birth.
And two of the seven
From out the weeping heaven
Flown sad, in sympathy
And wondering tears, to see
The dread sublimity
Of rugged Calvary,
Stayed sentinels and kept
The tomb where Jesus slept—
The loveliest of the sky,
Who gave himself to die.

And their rejoicing eyes
Beheld the Savior rise
And saw the earliest ray
Of that first Easter day !

" As, in God's economies,
What once is true, forever is,
And truth for angels holds for men,
So, evermore, as when
To watching spirits came
The primal Easter flame,
The best of honors given
To man, before his heaven,
He wins who faithful waits
With Right through cruel fates.
Who bides with Worth through shame
Shall have a lustrous fame ;
With Christ through night of scorn,
The joy of Easter morn ! "

Know this, ye troubled, know
That in the hour of woe,

Some angel waits above
Commissioned by the Love
Supreme, to fly and prove
With blessings from the skies,
That He is kind and wise
And doth permit the stress,
To give Him chance to bless
And those who suffer, place
To struggle into grace
Of goodness and the dower
Of perfectness of power.
Whoso behaveth right,
Whatever be his plight ;
Whoever thinketh bright,
Important, happy thing
To say, or paint, or sing,
Hath influence from the sky,
And voice to ask him try
To make both fine and strong
The word, the tint, the song,
Who heeds the first, gains more
Of the celestial store
That gives uplift from trite
To new, from slough to height,
From weakness unto might,

From dryness, deadness, blight,
To bud, and leaf, and bloom,
That hint of Junes to come.
O gracious boundlessness
Of Heaven's power to bless !

Seen or invisible,
As seemeth to them well,
The spirits come to tell
The words of wrath or love
That emanate above.
And, though alert to sounds
And sights that vexed their rounds,
The guardsmen of the mines,
Sworn to the czar's designs,
Saw not those whose emprise
Was threatening from the skies,
Though came they bright as stars
To speak the doom of czars.
But read the guards in mine
The deeply-written sign,
And sent a message far
To citadel of czar.
And he to frenzy flew,
That quick to fury grew.

Imperial mandate given,
The royal guards had striven
The writing to erase.
But none could yet efface
Indictment graven there
By one of upper air.
And livid in that mine
Fierce glistened still each line :
" *Unless the czars repent*
Before the firmament
And right the wrong
Their hate hath done so long,
For Poland's cup of gall
The Russian throne must fall ! "

The czar a chemist sent,
Who with fierce caustics went,
To eat the message out
That so had put to rout
The pleasure of the czar,
And toiled from dawn to star
With fiery rust and bar.

Homeward the chemist flew,
And this the message true :
" No science can begin,
Nor skill, the race to win—
The words are burning in ! "
Some straying peasant heard
The courier's fateful word
Reported to the lord
Chief courtier of the king ;
And all the people sing,
And children join the din,
" *The words are burning in !* "

Again the man with bar
And rust to please the czar,
And tear the message out,
Of which the people shout.
And with his mission o'er,
Reports he as before :
" A span, a foot, a rod—
Swift science doth but plod.
The words do inward fly
As missioned from the sky ! "

In rage the monarch flew,
The alchemist he slew,
And sent another, still,
With threat to chain and kill,
Did he not burn or tear
That message of despair.
And with him fared a guard
That no one should retard,
Nor scientist should flee,
If unsuccessful he.
Returned, he trembling said,
As forth the guardsmen led
Him, strongly held and bound,
To slay if faithless found ;
" A foot, an ell, a rod—
The message writ of God
About a nation's sin
Is further burning in ! "
The guardsmen aim to fire !
The monarch cries, " Retire
With him in heavy chains
To wildest northern plains !
The recreant's mocking breath
.Must not the ease of death ! "

Fruitless the despot's plan
Of banishing the man.
Borne by the ready airs,
His message onward fares,
Through scenes of joy and dearth,
Around the peopled earth !
Hill tells it unto fen,
The wilds to homes of men,
The mountain to the moor,
The robin at the door
Of cottage and of hall—
That broken soon the thrall
Of Russian slaves will be,
And joy of Liberty !

And chant the brooks and birds :
" The angel-written words
About a nation's sin
Are ever burning in ! "
And other birds are singing
In every morn of winging,
In every moon of flying
For food for birdlings crying,
And eve of homeward hieing

To nest, and rest, and love,
A message from above
Befitting lark or dove
To sing in all the earth :
" Man's greatest wealth, his worth,
His unearned plenty, dearth ;
His best of liberty,
Deserving to be free."

Still other birds that fly
And sing, they know not why,
Thus cheer, inspire and warn
At eve and happy morn ;
" Whatever first success,
What flatterers address,
How fondly love caress,
How praiseth selfishness
That hopes return, to bless,
Whatever is the stress
Of noyance that doth press,
War waged for wrong is wrong,
And weak and never strong.
And weak is war for might ;
But ever finds true knight

That strong is war for right,
For God is in the fight !
Though right should lose the fray,
And victory delay,
Yet surely comes the day
Of victory, to stay,
And show that right hath might ;
For God is in the fight ! "

A WARNING TO COLUMBIA.

BUT briefly where it sung
   The sentient glowing hung.
Then over seas it came,
The fearless warning flame,
And o'er Potomac's tide
In indignation cried,
As, eyeing halls of state,
Mid-air the burning sate,
Self-poised in conscious truth
And sense of lasting youth :
" For shame, Columbia, shame !
Bedimming thy bright name

By leaguing with the power
That claims by heavenly dower
Each individual soul
Of realm in his control,
With right to dominate,
Unto severest fate
Those bending not the knee
At nod of Tyranny !

" Why dost thou promise, why,
That when to thee shall fly
Those fortunate to break
Their bondage and to take
Across the seas their way,
West guided by the ray
Of freedom, to thy land,
They shall be held for hand
Of czar, whose wrath they flee
To fly in hope to thee ?
These sent to despot back,
To dungeon and to rack,
For holding but the thought
That ill the monarchs wrought
Who joyed to curse
With an oppression worse

Than the tyrannic crimes
Of old barbaric times !
In league, Columbia, why,
With Russian tyranny ? "

In silence, then, the flame,
To hear if answer came
From out Columbian hall.
And, saying " Deaf to all,
And to thy past untrue ! "
The lustre, sighing, flew
To welcome of the blue,
That bent, sad questioning,
And bade the birds to sing,
And brooks—" Columbia, why
In league with tyranny ? "

ORDEAL AND OUTCOME.

O PATRIOTS, pure and strong,
    And waiting now so long,
And patiently, to see
The morn of liberty,
Wait on, for God doth wait !

For Christ, when in the fate
O'er which all nature wept
And Heaven sad vigils kept,
His slayers could forgive,
And died that they might live.
He shed in death the tears
That permeate the years,
And ever plead with man
The beauty of the plan
Of giving bread for blows,
For thorn, the thornless rose
Of love, that sweeter grows
Through trials oft and sore,
That, wounded, o'er and o'er,
Doth from its fragrant store
The balm of good disburse,
And blessings breathe for curse.

To keep this code of heaven,
Ye patriots have forgiven,
In hope that kindness win
Who seventy times should sin.
But seven times that have striven
These foes of man and Heaven,

And by ten thousand times
Have multiplied their crimes.
And ye forgive and wait,
Enduring still your fate.
And Heaven impatient grows,
And, noting long the woes
Of Poland and of all
Within the Russian's thrall,
Will surely send a hand,
To write where tyrant band,
In revel o'er their wine,
Shall read and know the sign
Grim glistening on the wall,
That tyranny must fall !
Aye, patience may endure ;
But wrath deferred is sure.
And soon the man shall rise
To hear and heed the cries
Of victims of the czars.
And then, O waiting stars,
How will ye shout and sing
And call the birds to wing
In swiftest flight, to tell
Wherever patriots dwell,

His name who conquered Tyranny
And set the exiles free,
And Poland's flag unfurled
To honor in the world.

Aye, God will heed the cries
Of Poland's agonies.
For, though His name is Love,
And His the carrier dove,
Yet His the eagle is,
And all the majesties
Of all the life of earth,
Since far creation's birth !
He gave the tiger power,
And ocean monsters dower,
To lash the seas to rage
And mighty ships engage.
He taught the earth to quake,
And made the mountains shake.
'Twas He created light
And piled the Alpine height.
He set the rhythmic spheres
To cadence of the years
Of the eternity
He gave the right to be !

His Christ of Olivet
And Galilee used, yet,
A scourge ; His Moses saw
The lightnings of the law
From Sinai blaze, to tell
That with Jehovah dwell
All powers, and it is well
With those alone who fear
Him, and in truth sincere,
Hold all His statutes dear,
Who live for righteousness,
And never to oppress.
And He, if stubborn prove
The czars to pleas of love,
Will call some iron man
To execute His plan,
To thunder forth His wrath
And plow with war a path
Through tyranny's domains
And break the exiles' chains,
And lead each patriot band
To home and native land.

And yet, protesting rhyme
Against the Russian crime,

Fail not his worth to sing,
Who, once in Russia king,
Had righted much of wrong,
Had not the furious throng
Smote Alexander down
And set the Russian crown
Against the Polish cause
Of Liberty's good laws.
And Polish patriots see
A crime in anarchy.
No vengeance on their foes
Would they ; but thornless rose
And white, and every flower
Of Peace for those whose power
Hath been so long the ban
Of Poland and of man !
Unselfish in their grief,
These patriots seek relief
For all who feel
The tyrant's iron heel.
To people of the realm
They seek to give the helm
Of Russian power,
As rightful dower.
Nor charge they the rod
Of tyranny to God.

And spurn they the extremes
Of the ill-visioned dreams
Of those anarchic fools
Whom wild unwisdom rules,
They of that base alloy
Which nerves men to destroy.

A PILGRIMAGE OF CZARS.

WILL tyrants turn who make
    Their chief delight to break
The patriotic heart,
And name their crime an art !
Yet grant imagination scope,
And patience chance to hope
That czars be won to sense
Of need of penitence,
Or scourged until they see
How wrong the cruelty
That gives to Poland tears
And damns a thousand years !
Should miracle be done,
The greatest under sun

The visioned stars have seen,
And czars repentance mean—
Go, czars, by conscience sent,
Go, honored to repent,
Go, with your burden bent,
Go any way ye must,
Go, if through thorns and dust ;
Go, if with heavy chains
Like exiles o'er the plains !
Go, grateful that you may ;
Go, seek fit place to pray.
Go where the zephyrs say
That sigh from heaven's way !
Go, foes of liberty,
And fall on suppliant knee
Where dust of Kracut is
'Mid Cracow's mysteries,
The first of Polish kings
The muse of history sings,
The Slavic chief of time
Ere czars had cursed his clime.
There, pleading not the claim
Of royalty or fame,
But only His good name
Who gave the one relief
That owned himself a thief—

There tell the skies your sin,
Aware, as ye begin,
That Christ, the ever kind,
With justice mild, consigned
To millstone and the sea
The unwept tyranny
Of Pharisees of old,
To whom ye likeness hold !
Kneel, then, in Cracow, where
The soul of Wanda fair
Doth frequent still the air
Above the hill that claims
Sweetest of Polish names.
And ask you there of Heaven
If czars can be forgiven !

BY KOSCIUSKO'S DUST.

THEN, with this pleading done,
   If beams benignant sun,
Or if for you there shine
One ray of star benign,
Then seek another grave,
His place whom Heaven gave,

To show to czars and earth
A Polish patriot's worth,
And sent to aid, in youth,
Columbia's cause of truth.

There, by this hero's rest,
See, if, with prayer addressed
The Heaven of Liberty,
Czars can forgiven be
Of Heaven and of the free !
There hear from far the cry
Of those who hope, or try
To hope, before they die,
To see once more the home
From which dear memories come.
O ! memories that burn,
And into torments turn !
How must the exiles yearn
For once to grasp the hand
Of kindred in the land
Of their great leader's birth,
The dearest land of earth !
O, cruel tyranny !
That freemen may not see
For once the boyhood farm,
Sweet with the pet brook's charm ;

For once the childhood cot,
For once the play-place grot,
For once the daisied mead,
For once two paths to lead,
As once, to trysting place
Of bravery and of grace !
For once the grassy mound
That love's fair roses crowned !
There's Linka's ashes lie,
Who had the choice to die
Or tell's the tyrant's spy,
When by His Highness bid,
Of patriot Pavel hid !

And there's the outlook hill,
And there the near-by rill,
And there the other stream,
Whose unforgotten gleam
Inspired the boyhood dream
Of busy, stirring life,
Of joy in hardest strife,
Of earning high success
And coming home to bless,
With nobly won largess,

The village where in joy
Erstwhile dwelt the boy !
Instead, condemned to pine,
Imprisoned in a mine,
For that high quality
That fits men to be free !

There, where the good man lies,
Best of the sanctities
Of the Sarmatian land,
There, tyrants, stand,
There, tyrants, kneel,
And well the honor feel !
There, ye who give a slave
The right to choose his grave,
The felon, who atones,
With hempen halter, groans
He caused, the right to say
Where ye his bones shall lay—
There, by Kosciusko's dust,
Be honest once, and just !
There, talk, repentant czars,
With conscience and the stars,
The eyeing stars, that see
What is sincerity,

And will no fleeting mood
Of tears for years of blood !
Tell stars and conscience why
In vain do freemen cry
To you for boon of serf,
For one green stretch of turf,
Where, from foreign strand
Sent back to native land—
Where, if not given breath
At home, they may at death
Be sent to final rest,
To slumber unoppressed !

Cannot endure the stars ?
Why, there's a place, ye czars,
Where stars do never shine,
And whence no royal line
Or peasant cometh back
By straight or devious track—
But onward still must fare
Whoever goeth there !
And there's another, too,
Where stars are never due,
But lurid lightnings glare,
And demons rule the air ;

And hither none shall fare
That ever enter there !
And there's another, still,
Of flowery plain and hill
Of Sion, blest abode
Of angels and of God !
And of the saints who rise
From earth's hard agonies
To freedom of the skies !
But, untransformed by grace
To fitness for the place,
In heaven no tyrants live ;
For heavenly blisses give
Such influence that 'twere hell
For tyrants there to dwell.

WARNINGS FROM ELDER DAYS.

O VAIN, presuming stars,
    Why contradict the czars !
For they have lived to see
Too much of history
To deign to a reply
When even Russians lie !

Boast not your hosts in arms,
That give the world alarms.
For steel-clad giants are
But pigmies to a star.
Stars laugh at all your power
And point to Shinar's tower,
That was, and Babylon,
That boasted to the sun
Of her Chaldean might !
And held the world in fright,
And perished in a night !
And but her ruins tell
Of Babylon that fell !

And point the stars to king
Of whom but furies sing,
The Herod throned of yore,
But cursed forever more
In street and cloister lore.

From scanning these
Look back to Rameses,

Who and whose like gave tears
For twice two hundred years
To chosen sons of God.
And these condemned to plod,
Scourged by oppression's rod
That grew by gore,
These, through their bondage sore,
Upon God's promise fed,
Till, brave enough, they fled,
By visioned shepherd led.

And now the sea before
Withholds from freedom's shore,
And prisoning mountains stand,
To hold for Pharoah's hand.
But look ! the flood divides,
Heaven holds apart the tides !
The fugitives pass through ;
Menephtah's hosts pursue.
But fierce returning waves
Whelm in their watery graves
Ruler, horsemen, all—
A wreck that hints the fall
Of the Egyptian throne,
O'er which, in warning moan,

The ages sweep, to say
That tyrants pass away !

Man's title to be free
Is writ in history.
And nature, too, decries
The despot's tyrannies.
In waking life of spring,
When glad the robins sing ;
In the persuasive breath
Of June from flowery heath ;
In airs that sweeten shade
Of pleasant wooded glade
And move the fairy ferns
To dance by merry burns ;
In storms around the peaks
Where fierce the thunder speaks ;
In chill November's gale
That sweeps the frosted vale ;
In Ocean's sullen roar
On Winter's icy shore—
In all her ministries,
The voice of nature is
Rebuke of tyrannies.

In tender tones and mild
As plaintive voice of child,
In clarion peal, and strong
As burst of lyric song ;
Commanding, deep and slow
As centuries that flow
Through history
Toward eternity—
The olden warning word,
Repeated, now is heard
In all the upward trend
To Consummation's end ;
The word in every wind,
The word in every mind,
But yours, audacious czars,
Who contradict the stars—
Let ye my people go !
Let ye the exiles go !

www.ingramcontent.com/pod-product-compliance
Lightning Source LLC
Chambersburg PA
CBHW021108020726
47500CB00003B/651